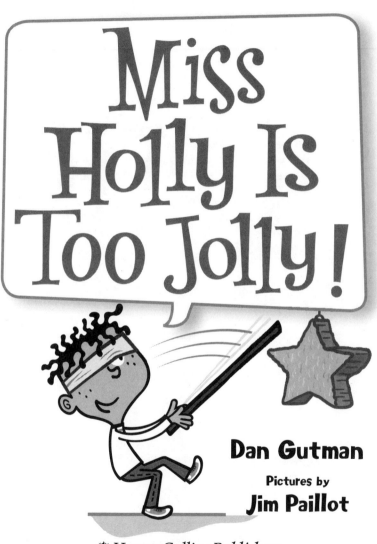

Miss Holly Is Too Jolly!

Dan Gutman

Pictures by
Jim Paillot

HarperCollins*Publishers*

Library of Congress Cataloging-in-Publication Data is available.

ISBN-10: 0-06-085382-4 (pbk.) — ISBN-13: 978-0-06-085382-2 (pbk.)

ISBN-10: 0-06-085383-2 (lib. bdg.) — ISBN-13: 978-0-06-085383-9 (lib. bdg.)

1 2 3 4 5 6 7 8 9 10

❖

First Edition

15·90

To Emma

Contents

Christmas, Hanukkah, and Kwanzaa

"Me llamo A.J. y odio la escuela."

That's "My name is A.J. and I hate school" in Spanish.

Miss Holly translated it for me. She's the Spanish teacher at Ella Mentry School.

"It's not fair," I said as our class walked down the hall to the language lab. "Why do we have to learn a whole nother language?"

"'Nother' isn't a word, Arlo," said Andrea Young. "You can't even speak *English* correctly."

Andrea is this girl in my class with curly brown hair who thinks she knows everything. She calls me by my real name because she knows I hate it.

"'Nother' is *too* a word," I told her.

"Is not."

"Is too."

We went back and forth like that for a while. Andrea said she looked up "nother" in the dictionary once, and it wasn't there. She's probably the only kid in the world who keeps a dictionary on her desk so she can look up words and show everybody how smart she is.

"'*Another*' is a word," Andrea said, "but not 'nother.'"

"Oh yeah?" I said. "If 'nother' isn't a word, then why did you just say it?"

Nah-nah-nah boo-boo on her.

Andrea was wearing this dumb hat that she made all by herself in her knitting class. Andrea takes classes in everything. She probably even takes a class in how to be annoying, because that's the one thing she's good at.

After walking a million hundred miles, we finally got to the language lab. What a dumb name. Labs are supposed to have test tubes and mad scientists and hunch-backed guys named Igor who limp. Our language lab is just a plain old room where we learn Spanish. What's up with that?

"Isn't learning Spanish fun?" Andrea said to her crybaby friend Emily. "I hope Miss Holly teaches us—"

She didn't get the chance to finish her sentence because at that very second Miss Holly danced in the door.

Miss Holly was playing a guitar and she had a big basket of fruit on her head. She was singing some crazy song and spinning around and stamping her feet. Her

red dress had pic-
tures of reindeer on
the back. On the front
were blinking lights
and the words "Happy
Holidays!"

When she finished the
song, Miss Holly yelled,
"Olay!" which is the name
of the stuff my mom
smears on her face at night.

"*¡Feliz Navidad!*" Miss Holly said.
"Happy Hanukkah! *Kwanzaa Yenu Iwe
Na Heri!*"

"What the heck does that mean?" I
asked.

"That means Merry Christmas, Happy Hanukkah, and Happy Kwanzaa!" Miss Holly replied.

"Which holiday do *you* celebrate?" asked Emily.

"Me?" said Miss Holly. "I celebrate *all* of them!"

If you ask me, it was a little early to be talking about the holidays. I mean, we just came back to school from Thanksgiving break a few days ago. Miss Holly is *too* jolly.

"I love all the holidays!" Miss Holly said. "I can't wait for December!"

"My favorite holiday is Halloween," said Neil, who everybody calls the nude kid, even though he wears clothes.

"My favorite holiday is Thanksgiving," said my friend Ryan, who will eat anything, even stuff that is not food.

"My favorite holiday is my birthday," said my other friend Michael, who never ties his shoes.

Everybody started shouting out their favorite holiday.

"What's *your* favorite holiday, A.J.?" Miss Holly asked me.

"My favorite holiday is Take Our Daughters to Work Day," I said.

"That's for *girls*," Andrea said. "Why is that *your* favorite holiday, Arlo?"

"Because *you're* not here," I replied.

"That's mean!" Andrea said. She crossed her arms and wrinkled up her face.

She was right. It *was* mean. That's why I said it!

I hate her.

Weird Words

2

"¡*Hola!*" Miss Holly said. "Today we're going to learn Spanish vocabulary words."

"Yay!" said the girls.

"Boo!" said the boys.

"The first word is 'toupee,'" said Miss Holly.

I know what a toupee is. It's fake hair that guys wear so they won't look bald. Our principal, Mr. Klutz, should get one because he's as bald as a bowling ball.

"The Spanish word for 'toupee' is *el peluquín*," said Miss Holly.

"*El peluquín*," we all repeated.

"Good," said Miss Holly. "The next word is 'lifeguard.' The Spanish word for 'lifeguard' is *el salvavidas*."

"*El salvavidas*," we all repeated.

"Good," said Miss Holly. "The next word is 'toilet.' The Spanish word for 'toilet' is *el inodoro*."

"*El inodoro*," we all repeated.

This was getting weird. I figured Miss

Holly would teach us words we'd use every day, like "When do we eat?" or "Where is the skate park?" But she was teaching us weird words instead.

Neil the nude kid raised his hand. "Why do we need to learn *those* words?" he asked.

"Well," said Miss Holly, "what if you're at the beach and you need to tell somebody that the lifeguard's toupee fell in the toilet?"

Miss Holly is weird.

"Okay, that's enough vocabulary for now," Miss Holly said.

"Let's learn how they celebrate the holidays in a Spanish-speaking country like Mexico!"

Miss Holly told us that eleven days after Christmas in Mexico, kids put their shoes out on the balcony before they go to sleep. If they've been good, their shoes will be filled with treats when they wake up the next morning.

"Eww, that's disgusting!" I said. "I wouldn't eat those smelly treats!"

Miss Holly said that was silly. Then she told us that for nine days before

Christmas in Mexico, people act out the journey of Mary and Joseph going to Bethlehem. After a big feast, they play the piñata game.

"Repeat after me," said Miss Holly. "Piñata!"

"Piñata," we all repeated.

I knew what a piñata was because Ryan had one at his birthday party. It's this big, hollow, paper thing you hang from a tree, and kids take turns whacking it with a stick. When the piñata breaks open, candy falls out and everybody grabs it.

Piñatas are cool because you get to do two very cool things—eat candy and whack something with a stick.

Miss Holly went to the closet, and guess what she took out?

I'm not going to tell you.

Okay, okay, I'll tell you.

A piñata! It was in the shape of a star. We were going to play the piñata game! All right!

Miss Holly climbed up on her desk and tied the piñata to a bar on the ceiling.

"Can I go first?" we all yelled.

Miss Holly said we'd go in ABC order, which meant that Andrea (AN) got to go first. I lined up behind her because my real name, Arlo, begins with AR.

Miss Holly told us that in Mexico the kids are blindfolded when they play the piñata game. She tied a blindfold over Andrea's eyes and put a stick in her hand.

"You can do it, Andrea!" the girls yelled.

"I bet she misses the whole thing," I told Ryan.

Well, Andrea was totally pathetic. She hardly *ever* hit the piñata. Even when she did, she only tapped it a little and it just spun around. All the boys were cracking up.

Finally it was my turn. Miss Holly tied the blindfold over my eyes and put the stick in my hand.

"Kill it, A.J.!" the boys yelled.

No way was I going to let anybody laugh at *me*. I was going to whack that piñata so hard, candy would fly all over the room. I reached back and swung the stick as hard as I could.

But I must have missed.

"Owwww!" somebody screamed.

I took off the blindfold. Emily was lying on the floor with her hands over her head.

"A.J. hit me!" she yelled.

"It was an accident!" I said. I must admit I've always *wanted* to hit Emily with a stick, but I would never do it on purpose. It wasn't *my* fault that she got so close.

Miss Holly gasped. "Go to Mrs. Cooney's office," she told Emily. Mrs. Cooney is the school nurse.

Emily went running out of the room, shrieking like an elephant fell on her. What a crybaby! She wasn't even bleeding or anything.

I thought Miss Holly was going to let

me have another turn, but she said the piñata game was too dangerous to play in school. Bummer in the summer!

It wasn't fair. We didn't even get any candy.

Santa Klutz Is Coming to Town

"Line up in ABC order," said our teacher, Miss Daisy, after we finished pledging the allegiance the next morning. "We're having an assembly!"

"Yay!" said the girls.

"Boo!" said the boys.

Assemblies are when the whole school

goes to the all-purpose room and we have to listen to somebody talk for a million hundred hours. The last time we had an assembly, some children's book author told us about his books. What a bore! The reading specialist, Mr. Macky, is always trying to get us to read.

I hate reading.

But this assembly looked like it was going to be different. The all-purpose room was decorated with big candy canes, snowmen, and fake snow. "Jingle Bells" was playing on the loudspeaker.

After we sat down, the most amazing thing in the history of the world happened. Something started coming down from the ceiling above the stage!

At first we couldn't tell what it was. Then we saw it was a sleigh! As it got lower, we could see Santa Claus sitting in the sleigh. Some kids were pulling long ropes that lowered the sleigh down until it reached the stage.

"Ho ho ho!"

"It's Santa Claus!" everybody shouted.

"I'm not Santa Claus," the guy said. He took off his Santa hat so we could see his shiny bald head. "I'm Santa KLUTZ!"

It was Mr. Klutz, the principal! Everyone started hooting and hollering. Miss Daisy shushed us. Mr. Klutz waited until everybody was quiet. He picked up a microphone so we could hear him better.

"I always gets santamental around the holidays," Mr. Klutz said. "Get it? *Santa* mental?"

"Hahahahahahahahahaha!"

We all laughed even though Mr. Klutz didn't say anything funny. When the principal makes a joke, you should always laugh. That's the first rule of being a kid. If you don't laugh at the principal's jokes, he'll get mad and lock you in the dungeon down in the basement.

"But seriously," Mr. Klutz said, "what do you get when you cross a snowman with a vampire?"

"What?" we all yelled.

"Frostbite!" he said. "Get it? Frost? Bite?"

"Hahahahahahahaha!"

Mr. Klutz is always cracking jokes. He thinks he is a real comedian. But his jokes are terrible. It should be against the law for principals to tell jokes.

"Do you know why Santa's little helper was depressed?" Mr. Klutz asked.

"Why?" we all yelled.

"Because he had low elf-esteem. Get it? Elf? Esteem?"

"Hahahahahaha!"

Maybe if we stopped laughing at his jokes, Mr. Klutz would stop telling them.

"What do you call people who are afraid of Santa?" Mr. Klutz asked.

"What?" we all yelled.

"Claustrophobic!" he said. "Get it? Claus? Trophobic?"

"Hahahaha!"

It was horrible. It was like watching one of those movies that never ends. I looked over at Ryan and Michael. They rolled their eyes.

"What do snowmen eat for breakfast?" Mr. Klutz asked.

"What?" we all yelled.

"Snowflakes!" he said. "Get it? Snow? Flakes?"

"Haha!"

Finally Mr. Klutz ran out of jokes. What a relief! He told us he was dressed up like Santa because he had big news. This year Ella Mentry School would be putting on its first ever holiday pageant. That's a show all about the holidays.

"Our art teacher, Ms. Hannah, will help paint the scenery. Our music teacher, Mr. Loring, will help with the songs. Our librarian, Mrs. Roopy, will help with the research. And the director of the pageant," Mr. Klutz announced, "will be our own . . . Miss Holly!"

Everybody clapped, and Miss Holly danced up onto the stage with her guitar. She played "Winter Wonderland," and we all joined in.

"I'm so excited!" Miss Holly said. "We're going to sing songs, perform skits, and have lots of fun. It's going to be the best holiday pageant ever!"

It sounded horrible.

Secret Santa

After the assembly we walked a million hundred miles back to our class. Andrea was all excited about the holiday pageant. She loves to be in plays because she's a big show-off.

"Last year I was in *The Nutcracker*," she bragged.

"They made a play about nuts?" I asked. "No wonder *you* were in it."

Andrea got all mad. "Why do you have to be so mean, Arlo?"

"Why do you have to be so annoying?" I asked.

"Enough chitchatting," Miss Daisy said when we were all sitting in our seats. "I have some important news. This year we're going to have a Secret Santa in our class."

Secret Santa? Who's that? None of us had ever heard of Secret Santa. But Santa is cool, and anything that involves secrets is cool. So Secret Santa must be cool.

Miss Daisy told us that she wrote everyone's name on slips of paper and put them all into a fishbowl. Each of us would take a slip of paper out of the fishbowl, and then we'd have to get a present for that kid. But we couldn't tell the kid we were getting them a present. That's what made it a *secret.* Miss Daisy said we would exchange our Secret Santa presents in a few weeks, just before the big holiday pageant. If anyone forgot to bring in a present, they wouldn't be allowed to *get* a present either.

Everybody was all excited. We lined up to pick slips of paper out of the fishbowl. I hoped I wouldn't pick some lame girl like Andrea or Emily. I'd rather get a present for Ryan or Michael or one of the other boys.

We lined up in ZYX order, which is the opposite of ABC order. Everybody picked a slip of paper out of the fishbowl and giggled a little when they saw the name on it. Finally it was my turn. There were only a couple of slips of paper left.

"No peeking, A.J.," Miss Daisy told me

as I reached my hand into the fishbowl.

I picked out a slip of paper.

I looked at the paper.

The paper said . . .

I'm not going to tell you.

Okay, okay, I'll tell you.

The paper said, "Emily."

Noooooooooooooooooooooooo!

Not Emily! What could I possibly get for Emily? She is a real girly-girl. I will have to go to some girly-girl store and buy some girly-girl present like smelly perfume. It will be horrible.

Secret Santa is stupid.

Learning How to Speak Spanish

A few days later, we were in the language lab and Miss Holly was telling us all about Spain. It's a country in Europe, and it's the whole way across the Atlantic Ocean.

Miss Holly played her guitar, sang, tap-danced, and told us all kinds of useless information about Spain. Did you know that Spain is twice the size of Oregon? I didn't know that.

Do you care?

Me neither.

"In Spain," Miss Holly told us, "boys and girls only have to go to school until they are sixteen years old."

"All right!" I said. "I'm moving to Spain!"

"Then you'll have to learn to speak Spanish, A.J.," said Miss Holly.

I told her I already know how to speak Spanish because I saw this movie called *Terminator II* where Arnold Schwarzenegger kills a bunch of guys, and before he leaves he says, "*Hasta la vista*, baby!" My mom told me that means "until we meet again." It was a

cool movie.

"That's good, A.J., but you'll have to learn a lot more than that," Miss Holly said. "Let's work on our Spanish vocabulary for the pageant."

"Yay!" said the girls.

"Boo!" said the boys.

"The first word we're going to learn

today is 'nose,'" said Miss Holly. "The Spanish word for 'nose' is *la nariz*," said Miss Holly.

"La nariz," we all repeated.

"Good," said Miss Holly. "The next word is 'think.' The Spanish word for 'think' is *pensar*."

"Pensar," we all repeated.

"Good," said Miss Holly. "The next word is 'Christmas tree.' The Spanish word for 'Christmas tree' is *el árbol de Navidad*."

"El árbol de Navidad," we all repeated.

"Good," said Miss Holly. "The next word is 'stuck.' The Spanish word for 'stuck' is *pegado*."

"Pegado," we all repeated.

Miss Holly sure picks weird words.

Neil the nude kid raised his hand. "Why do we need to learn those words?" he asked.

"Well," Miss Holly said, "what if you're in Spain and you need to say, 'I think I have a Christmas tree stuck to my nose'?"

Miss Holly is weird.

The Opposite of Hanukkah

During the first week in December, Miss Daisy told us all about the holidays so we'd be ready for the pageant. I already knew the story of Christmas. But I didn't know much about Hanukkah.

Now, I don't remember *everything* Miss Daisy told us. But basically, Hanukkah has something to do with a war. I know all about war. I have some plastic army guys down in my basement, and me and Michael and Ryan line them up and shoot them with rubber bands.

Anyway, a million hundred years ago, the Jewish people were fighting a war. They were way outnumbered by another army, but they kicked their butts anyway. So after the war was over, the Jewish people went back to their temple to hang out and play video games and stuff. It was dark out. They didn't have lightbulbs in those days, so they had to light oil lamps or they would bump into the walls when they walked into the kitchen to get more pizza.

The problem was that they could only find one jar of oil. That would last one night, but they wanted to hang out all week playing video games and eating pizza. I guess they sent somebody to the gas station to get more oil, but he never came back. So they put the one jar of oil they had into the lamp and lit it.

The cool thing is that the oil didn't just last one night. It didn't just last two nights. It didn't just last three nights. It lasted eight whole nights! It was a miracle!

"Wow!" we all said after Miss Daisy finished telling us the story of Hanukkah.

"I saw a miracle like that once," I said.

"Tell us about it, A.J.," said Miss Daisy.

"We were driving to my grandmother's house," I said. "Suddenly our car stopped right in the middle of the highway. My dad said he thought he had a full tank of gas, but it turned out the gas gauge was broken, and the tank was empty."

"That doesn't have anything to do with Hanukkah," Andrea said.

"Sure it does," I said. "The Jewish people thought they only had a little oil, but it turned out they had a lot. We thought we had a lot of gas, but we only had a little. It was the opposite of Hanukkah."

"You're a dumbhead," Andrea said.

"So is your face," I told her. Anytime somebody says something mean to you, all you have to do is say, "So is your face." That's the first rule of being a kid.

Miss Daisy told me and Andrea to

knock it off. She said that Hanukkah lasts for eight nights, and each night they light a candle in the menorah.

"They stick the candles in manure?" I asked. "That's disgusting!"

"Menor*ah*," Miss Daisy said. "It's like a candleholder."

"Oh," I said. "I knew that."

To celebrate Hanukkah, Jewish kids play this game with a four-sided top called a dreidel that spins around, and they eat potato pancakes called latkes, and they hunt for chocolate coins wrapped in gold foil. The kids get presents every night, too, of course. Hanukkah is cool.

Miss Daisy showed us how to spin a

dreidel and gave us each a piece of chocolate money. We had a bathroom break after that, and then she said it was time to work on our writing skills. We were learning to write friendly letters, so Miss Daisy asked us if we'd like to write letters to Santa Claus.

"Yeah!" everybody shouted.

She told us to write whatever we wanted. This is what I wrote:

Dear Santa,
Please bring me a dirt bike and a football and a skateboard and a remote-control car and that new video game where you get to kill zombies with machine guns. Also I need a new Striker Smith action figure because mine got run over by the school bus after Ryan threw it out the window. I'll take anything else you have lying around your workshop that is cool too. I love presents. But please don't bring me any boring stuff like clothes or books.

Miss Daisy looked at what I was writing and said I had to write something besides a list of stuff I want. So I added this:

Santa, I think you should lose some weight. On TV they keep saying that Americans weigh too much. Maybe if you worked more than one day a year, you would lose a few pounds. My mother lost twenty pounds on Weight Watchers. That might work for you.

Also, I don't think it was nice for the other reindeer to make fun of Rudolph, laughing and calling him names. That was mean. If I was Rudolph and they wouldn't let me play any

reindeer games, I would punch those
other reindeer in the nose.
    Sincerely,
    A.J.
    P.S. One more thing. Did you ever
hit your head on the North Pole?

Miss Daisy asked if anyone wanted to
read their letter in front of the class.
Andrea was the only one who raised her
hand (of course), so she stood up and
started reading.

Dear Santa,
    This year I don't want you to bring
me anything. There are children all
over the world who don't have any

toys. So please take the toys you were going to give to me and give them to poor children instead. The world would be a better place if people had less toys and more peace and love.

Love,

Andrea

What a brownnoser! I know for a fact that Andrea only said that stuff so Miss Daisy would like her. Once I went to Andrea's house for her birthday party, and the place was *filled* with toys. She has every American Girl doll ever made. The only reason Andrea doesn't want Santa to bring her any more toys is because she has no place to put them.

After Andrea finished reading her

dumb letter, the most amazing thing in the history of the world happened. Miss Daisy started crying!

"That's the most beautiful letter I've ever heard, Andrea," said Miss Daisy.

Andrea smiled her Little-Miss-Perfect smile.

Why doesn't a sack filled with letters fall on her head?

Is Santa Claus Real?

That afternoon me and Michael and Ryan were in the vomitorium eating lunch. Andrea and Emily and their girly friends were at the next table, so they couldn't bother us.

It's noisy in the vomitorium! Everyone was hooting and hollering. The lunch lady, Ms. LaGrange, was wearing these antler earmuff thingies on her head to block out the sound.

Ms. LaGrange is strange.

I had a peanut butter and jelly sandwich. Michael had a tuna sandwich. Ryan had two slices of bread and some slices of ham. Instead of putting the ham between the bread slices, he put it on the *outside* of the bread. Then he started eating.

"Why did you put the ham on the *outside* of your sandwich?" I asked him.

"It's not a sandwich," Ryan replied. "It's a wichsand."

Ryan is weird.

"I'll bet Santa isn't going to read those

letters we wrote," Michael said as he bit into his sandwich.

"Santa doesn't even exist," Ryan said. "One time I saw this Santa guy on the street ringing a bell, and then on the next block, there was *another* Santa guy who looked just like him."

"Maybe the second one was a clone," I said. "My friend Billy who lives around the corner told me that they can take a cell from a sheep and clone it into a whole nother sheep."

"'Nother' isn't a word, A.J.," Michael said.

"Neither is your face," I told him.

"Look, it's just impossible for one guy to visit every single house in the world in one night," Ryan said. "Besides, our house doesn't even have a chimney. How would he get in?"

"If you don't have a chimney," Michael

said, "Santa comes in through the toilet bowl. Everybody has one of them."

"That's disgusting," I said. "And he couldn't fit through the toilet anyway."

"It's just impossible," Ryan insisted. "There's no way Santa could make toys for every kid in the world."

"He has Elvis to help him," I said.

Michael and Ryan looked at me.

"Not *Elvis*, dumbhead!" Michael yelled, slapping his forehead. "Elves! He has *elves* to help him!"

"I knew that."

At the table beside us, Andrea and her annoying friends were giggling. They must have been listening in on our private conversation.

"You better watch out, Arlo," Andrea said. "Santa has a list, and he's checking it twice."

"He knows if you've been bad or good," said Emily, "so be good for goodness' sake."

"Who asked you two?" I said.

"You're naughty," Andrea said. "But Emily and I are nice, so Santa is going to bring us good presents. He's probably going to bring you a lump of coal."

"That's okay," I said. "I'll give it away to some poor boys and girls who don't have any coal. Then we'll have more peace and love in the world."

Ryan and Michael cracked up. Nah-nah-nah boo-boo on Andrea! Why doesn't a giant lump of coal fall on her head?

Getting Ready for the Holiday Pageant

"¡Buenos días!" Miss Holly said a few days later. That means "good day" in Spanish. There were red and green balloons and streamers all over the hallways. Spanish Christmas music was playing. And Miss Holly had that basket of fruit on her head again.

Everybody was excited about our first rehearsal for the big holiday pageant. Everybody except the boys, that is.

When we got to the language lab, Miss Holly was up on a ladder taping little plants to the walls.

"What's that?" asked Neil the

nude kid.

"It's mistletoe!" said Miss Holly.

What a dumb name. Missiles blast into outer space. How can a missile have a toe? They should definitely get a new name for that plant.

Miss Holly told us that when two people are standing under mistletoe, they're supposed to kiss. Eww! Yuck! Disgusting! I'm not kissing anyone. And I'm sure not going to kiss anyone just because some *plant* told me to. Mistletoe is creepy. I'm not going anywhere near that stuff.

Miss Holly told us that besides Christmas and Hanukkah, there is another holiday people celebrate in December. It's an African American holiday called Kwanzaa. Ryan got all excited, because that's the holiday his family celebrates. Miss Holly asked him to tell us about it.

Ryan told us that Kwanzaa means "first fruits," and it celebrates the harvest of the crops. It starts the day after Christmas and lasts seven days. Each day you light a candle in this candleholder called a *kinara*. Then somebody will say *"Harambee,"* which means "Let's pull together" in Swahili.

It wasn't fair. Christmas only lasts one day. But Kwanzaa lasts seven days and Hanukkah lasts eight days. Man, I wish I was black or Jewish.

Ryan told us that on *kuumba*, the sixth day of Kwanzaa, they have a big feast called *karamu*. They eat fried okra, vegetable stew, squash, peanut soup, and sweet potato pie. Yuck! Ryan will eat anything. If I had to eat that stuff, I'd die.

But other than eating that yucky food, Kwanzaa sounded cool. Ryan taught us a Kwanzaa song called "Kuumba," and Miss Holly said it would be perfect for the holiday pageant. Then Miss Holly told us that we were going to have to wear costumes and memorize lines. The holiday pageant was sounding lamer and lamer. She also said she needed to pick kids for the speaking parts. All the girls got excited.

"Oooh, can I be the sugar plum fairy?" begged Andrea.

"Oooh, can I sing the dreidel song?" begged Emily.

"What about you boys?" asked Miss Holly. "Which speaking parts do you want?"

"We don't want any speaking parts," I announced.

"That's right," agreed Michael and Ryan.

"I won't force you to take a speaking part," Miss Holly said, "but you do have to be in the pageant. You three boys will be the stage crew."

"Stage crew?" I asked. "What's that?"

"That means you'll work the spotlight and move the scenery and props around," said Miss Holly.

Being on the stage crew sounded cool. I looked at Ryan and Michael to make sure they thought so too.

"No problemo," I said. That's Spanish for "no problem," in case you don't speak Spanish as well as me.

"But I'll still need you to wear costumes," Miss Holly said, "because we need elves. We must have elves! You can't have a holiday pageant without elves!"

"We don't want to be elves!" Michael said. "Elves are lame."

"Yeah, I'm not dressing up like

an elf," I said.

Miss Holly looked at us, and I could tell that she was getting mad because she put her hands on her hips. Whenever grown-ups put their hands on their hips, that means they're mad. Nobody knows why.

I was afraid Miss Holly might punish us by making us be sugar plum fairies. Then

we'd have to wear tights like my sister. That's when I got the greatest idea in the history of the world.

"Instead of dressing up like elves," I said, "can we dress up like *Elvis?*"

Miss Holly thought it over for a few seconds.

"Okay!" she finally agreed. "You three boys can be Elvis!"

All right! Maybe the holiday pageant wouldn't be so lame after all.

The Most Horrible Thing in the History of the World

A couple of days later, around two o'clock, we came into the all-purpose room for rehearsal. Miss Holly was wearing a Santa Claus hat and beard. She's weird.

"Habari gani?" she said.

"What the heck does that mean?" I asked.

"That means 'What's the news?' in Swahili," said Miss Holly. "You say it during Kwanzaa."

It was a week before the big holiday pageant, and we had to rehearse every day. There was a lot of work to do. We had Christmas, Hanukkah, and Kwanzaa songs to learn, lines to memorize, and entrances and exits to practice.

Me and Ryan and Michael had to learn

how to move the scenery and props around and work the spotlight, too. At the end of the pageant, it would be our job to lower Santa Claus (Mr. Klutz, of course) and his sleigh down from the ceiling with ropes. That was going to be cool.

Miss Holly said that because we were Elvises, we could sing "Hound Dog," even though it didn't have anything to do with the holidays. Mr. Loring, our music teacher, played piano for all the songs. Miss Holly played her guitar.

Emily got to sing a solo. She is a big crybaby, but she has a pretty good voice, and Miss Holly let her sing "The Dreidel

Song." Emily was practicing it when I came up with the most brilliant idea in the history of the world.

"Since she's singing a song about a dreidel," I said to Miss Holly, "maybe she should spin around too?"

"Great idea, A.J.!" said Miss Holly.

I'm in the gifted and talented program, and I'm constantly coming up with genius ideas. I should get the No Bell Prize for that one.

At the end of rehearsal, Miss Holly told us how proud she was. She said the holiday pageant was going to be great. Miss Holly was so pleased that she told us she was going to invite Dr. Carbles, the president of the Board of Education, to come and see the show. Wow! If the principal is the king of the school, the president of the Board of Education must be like the king of the whole world.

We rehearsed until three o'clock, when it was time for dismissal. Then we lined up outside the doorway in ABC order. That's when Andrea turned around and whispered in my ear, "Hey, Arlo. Look up!"

I looked up.

It was that mistletoe stuff! It was hanging from the doorway right over our heads! How did it get up there?

I remembered what Miss Holly told us about mistletoe. If two people are under it, they're supposed to kiss. Andrea was standing there with her lips all puckered up like she was trying to whistle. Eww! Yuck! Disgusting! What is her problem?

No way was I going to kiss Andrea. I didn't know what to say. I didn't know what to do. I had to think fast. I looked around to see if Ryan and Michael were watching.

"You have to kiss me, Arlo," Andrea whispered.

"I do not."

"Do too."

"No way."

"Yes way."

"Not in my lifetime."

"It's the rule, Arlo."

"Says who?"

"If you don't kiss me, you'll be in trouble, Arlo."

I'd rather be in trouble than kiss Andrea. I'd rather be run over by a herd of buffalo than kiss Andrea. I'd rather have an elevator fall on my head than kiss Andrea. I'd rather *die*–

I didn't get the chance to finish my thought, because at that very moment the most horrible thing in the history of the world happened.

Andrea kissed *me*!

Ugh! On the lips! I thought I was gonna throw up! Quickly I wiped my lips off. I

mean, I wiped off my lips. I mean, my lips stayed on, but I wiped them off. What I'm trying to say is I didn't want to be infected by Andrea's disgusting cooties. I just hoped nobody saw what happened.

"Oooooh!" Ryan said. "Andrea and A.J. just kissed. They must be in *love!*"

"When are you gonna get married?" asked Michael.

If those guys weren't my best friends, I would hate them.

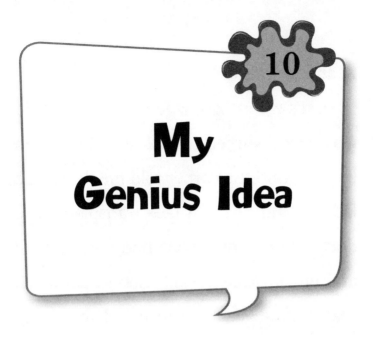

My Genius Idea

My life was over.

I ran home so fast I could have won a gold medal in the Olympics.

Now that Andrea had kissed me, going back to school was out of the question. I could never show my face there again. Ryan and Michael would never let me hear the end of it.

That's when I got a genius idea. I could get plastic surgery! My friend Billy who lives around the corner told me that some lady in France got a face transplant. The doctors just took somebody else's face and put it on her head. Cool! I could do that. I could get a new face and go back to school. Nobody would know it was me.

But getting a face transplant sounded disgusting. And my parents probably wouldn't get me one anyway. They wouldn't even get me a new Striker Smith action figure to replace the one Ryan threw out the bus window. No way were they going to get me a new face.

Now that Andrea had kissed me, I had no other choice. I had to move to Antarctica, where no human being would ever see me again. I would live with the penguins. Penguins are cool, and they wouldn't care that Andrea kissed me.

"Can you drive me to Antarctica?" I asked my mother after school. "I need to go live with the penguins for the rest of my life."

"Sure," she replied, "but first we have to go to the pet store."

Oh, I completely forgot! We were all out of fish food! My chore at home is to take care of our fish. Mom had told me first thing in the morning that after school we were going to the pet store to get fish food.

Mom says I have to do chores like feeding our fish because doing chores makes you a responsible person. That makes no sense at all. I'm *already* a responsible person. Any time something goes wrong, everybody says I'm responsible.

So we drove to the pet store. They have all kinds of animal stuff there. They even have Christmas presents for pets. People actually give gifts to their dogs!

Dog owners are weird.

You have to be real careful with fish. You have to feed them, clean their tank, and make sure the filter is working. I found the fish food and got in line with my mom to pay for it. There was a little sign in front of the cash register that said:

DID YOU FORGET ANYTHING?

Hmm, did I forget anything? That's when I suddenly remembered what I forgot. I forgot all about the Secret Santa present I was supposed to get for Emily! We had to bring them in tomorrow!

Oh, man! If I didn't bring in a Secret Santa present for Emily, I wouldn't get a present from *my* Secret Santa! And I *love* getting presents. I *had* to go back to school. If I went to Antarctica, I wouldn't get my Secret Santa present.

"Mom," I asked, "can you drive me to the mall after this?"

"I thought you wanted me to drive you to Antarctica."

"I changed my mind," I said. "I need to go to a smelly perfume store to get a Secret Santa present for Emily."

Mom was really mad. The stores are all crowded before Christmas, and the traffic is really bad. She said she didn't have time to take me to the smelly perfume store.

That's when I got another one of my genius ideas. I could get Emily a present right there at the pet store! They sell

goldfish for just ten cents. I could get
Emily a couple of goldfish. They would
make a way cooler present than smelly

perfume! And I wouldn't have to waste a lot of my money buying smelly perfume for that crybaby Emily, who I don't even like. The lady behind the counter even said she'd put the goldfish in a plastic bag filled with water and wrap it up in a box.

Haha! I'm a genius! That's why I'm in the gifted and talented program.

The Arrival of
Secret Santa

I was nervous about going to school the next morning. I wanted to get my Secret Santa present, but I didn't want the guys to make fun of me for getting kissed by Andrea. I decided to stay away from her, no matter what.

I put my backpack in my cubby. Ryan

and Michael didn't even mention anything about me kissing Andrea. I guess they forgot about it.

After we pledged the allegiance, everybody got all excited because it was time to open our Secret Santa presents.

Ryan got a jigsaw puzzle from his Secret Santa. Michael got Legos from his Secret Santa. Neil the nude kid got a model plane from his Secret Santa. I kept waiting for my turn.

"Who is A.J.'s Secret Santa?" Miss Daisy finally asked.

"I am!"

It was Andrea! Oh man! If I had known that Andrea was my Secret Santa, I would have moved to Antarctica.

"Oooooh!" Ryan said. "A.J. got a present from Andrea. She kissed him too. They must be in *love*!"

"When are you gonna get married?" asked Michael.

I told them to shut up. Andrea gave me the present. I tore off the wrapping paper and the dumb bow (which serves no purpose anyway). Then I opened the box. And do you know what was inside?

I'm not going to tell you.

Okay, okay, I'll tell you.

It was a hat.

A hat! Who gets a kid a hat? A hat isn't a present. A hat is clothes. It was horrible.

Not only that, but it looked just like the dumb hat Andrea wears all the time.

"I knitted it myself," Andrea said, "in my knitting class."

"How wonderful, Andrea!" said Miss Daisy. "A homemade present is so much nicer than something you buy in a store.

A.J., what do you say to Andrea?"

No way was I going to wear a hat that looked just like Andrea's dumb hat. I didn't know what to say. I didn't know what to do. I had to think fast.

"I hate hats," I said.

"You're mean!" Andrea said.

Miss Daisy made me apologize to Andrea, so I told her I was sorry she made me a dumb hat.

"Who is Emily's Secret Santa?" asked Miss Daisy.

"I am," I said.

I took out the present and gave it to Emily. I was so excited because my present was way cooler than all the others.

She opened it up.

"What is it?" everybody asked.

Emily pulled the plastic bag out of the box and started crying.

"It's a dead fish!" she sobbed. "I can't believe you got me a dead fish for Christmas, A.J.!"

"It wasn't dead when I *got* it!" I said. "And there were two of them. Where's the other one?"

"They must have eaten each other," said Ryan. "Stuff like that happens all the time with fish, you know."

"Man, that's twenty cents I wasted," I said.

"This is going to be a *terrible* Christmas," Emily cried as she went running out of the room, "and A.J. is responsible!"

See? I told you I was responsible.

The Big
Holiday Pageant

Finally the day of the big holiday pageant arrived. Everybody came to school in their costumes. Miss Holly wore a Santa suit. Me and Ryan and Michael wore black jackets and had our hair greased up so we looked like Elvis. It was cool.

We peeked through the curtains from

backstage. The all-purpose room was packed with parents. A bunch of them were setting up video cameras to record the show.

"Guess what?" Miss Holly said. "Dr. Carbles, the president of the Board of Education, is here! He's sitting in the front row! Let's put on a great show for him."

The stage was decorated with big candy canes, snowmen, fake snow, and a

giant reindeer. It looked great. Miss Holly nodded to me and Ryan and Michael. We pulled a long rope to open the curtain.

The show started out with one of the fifth-grade classes telling the story of Christmas. After that me and Michael and Ryan sang "Hound Dog." Everybody went crazy! After that one of the fourth-grade classes told the story of Kwanzaa. After that we sang "Winter Wonderland." After that one of the third-grade classes told the story of Hanukkah. After that Emily sang "The Dreidel Song."

"Dreidel, dreidel, dreidel, I made it out of clay. . . ."

Me and Michael and Ryan were taking

turns working the spotlight, and it was my turn. I shone the light on Emily while she sang and spun around.

"The light is too high, A.J.," Ryan said. "You're shining it in her eyes."

"I am not," I said.

"Are too," he said.

We went back and forth like that for a while, but we didn't get the chance to finish the argument, because the most amazing thing in the history of the world happened.

While Emily was singing and spinning around, she must have slipped on some fake snow or something because she fell off the stage! You should have been there! When Emily was falling, she tried to grab hold of the giant reindeer. But it wasn't nailed down or anything, and the two of them fell into the front row and landed on Dr. Carbles, the president of the Board of

Education! It was a real Kodak moment.

People were screaming. Mrs. Cooney, the nurse, ran over to make sure Emily was okay. The reindeer's head fell off, and some of the kindergarten kids started crying. It was hilarious. And we got to see it live and in person.

Miss Holly ran onto the stage and told the audience there would be a short intermission. Backstage, all the girls were upset. All the boys were laughing our heads off.

"This is the worst holiday pageant ever!" said Andrea. "And Arlo is responsible."

"Me?" I asked. "What did I do?"

"It was your idea for Emily to spin around," she said, "and you shined the spotlight in her eyes. That's why she fell off the stage. Now everything is a big mess!"

"So is your face," I told her.

Miss Holly said we should both calm down. She said the show was still great, and that we should get ready for the big finale. All the kids in the school were going to gather on the stage and sing "Jingle Bells" while Santa's Elvises (that's us) lowered Mr. Klutz and his sleigh full of presents down from the ceiling.

Everybody got into position. Mr. Klutz climbed into the sleigh in his Santa costume. Ryan pulled open the curtains. Me and Michael grabbed the ropes to lower the sleigh down from the ceiling. The parents started clapping.

"'Jingle Bells, jingle bells, jingle all the way . . .'"

Me and Michael pulled on the ropes. The only problem was, my rope was stuck.

"My rope is stuck!" I yelled over to Michael.

But he couldn't hear me over the music. He kept pulling his rope.

"'Oh what fun it is to ride in a one-horse

open sleigh—hey!'"

I looked up at the sleigh. The front of it was coming down, but the back part was stuck.

The sleigh was tilting forward. Mr. Klutz was going to fall!

I tried to get my rope loose, but it was still stuck. Michael kept lowering the front end of the sleigh. Mr. Klutz reached up and grabbed one of the poles on the ceiling.

"'Jingle Bells, jingle bells, jingle all the—'"

The kids didn't get the chance to finish their song because all the presents that were in the sleigh tumbled out and fell on their heads. Some of the parents started screaming. Mr. Klutz was hanging from the pole near the ceiling. I guess it was the North Pole. Hahaha!

"Help! Help!" he yelled.

Mr. Klutz's Santa hat and fake beard fell off. The beard

landed on some first grader's head. She freaked out and threw it into the audience. It landed on some lady. She screamed and threw it off her like it was a dead animal. It landed on some other lady, and she screamed too. The parents were throwing the beard around the all-purpose room. The custodian, Miss Lazar, ran to get a ladder so she could rescue Mr. Klutz.

"Those Elvises ruined the show!" some kid shouted.

I looked at Ryan. Ryan looked at Michael. Michael looked at me. We didn't have to say anything. The three of us made a run for the exit in the back of

the all-purpose room.

"It's Arlo's fault," Andrea hollered. "He's responsible!"

"The Elvises have left the building," Michael yelled as we ran out the door.

"*Hasta la vista,* baby!" I yelled.

We ran out of there as fast as we could.

I don't know if we'll ever go back.

Well, that's what happened at our big holiday pageant. Maybe me and Ryan and Michael will have to go live in Antarctica for the rest of our lives. Maybe Miss Holly will go live in Spain. Maybe the video of Emily falling off the stage will be on *America's Funniest Home Videos*. Maybe me and Ryan and Michael will be allowed to come back to school. Maybe we'll have a better holiday pageant next year. Maybe Miss Lazar will be able to get Mr. Klutz down from the North Pole.

But it won't be easy!